KIDS CAN'T ST??
THE CHOO??
OWN ADVENTU?? ??ORIES!

"Choose Your Own Adventure is the best thing that has come along since books themselves."
—Alysha Beyer, age 11

"I didn't read much before, but now I read my Choose Your Own Adventure books almost every night."
—Chris Brogan, age 13

"I love the control I have over what happens next."
—Kosta Efstathiou, age 17

"Choose Your Own Adventure books are so much fun to read and collect—I want them all!"
—Brendan Davin, age 11

And teachers like this series, too:

"We have read and reread, worn thin, loved, loaned, bought for others, and donated to school libraries our Choose Your Own Adventure books."

CHOOSE YOUR OWN ADVENTURE®—
AND MAKE READING MORE FUN!

Bantam Books in the Choose Your Own Adventure® Series
Ask your bookseller for the books you have missed

REVENGE OF THE RUSSIAN GHOST

BY JAY LEIBOLD

ILLUSTRATED BY STEPHEN MARCHESI

An R.A. Montgomery Book

BANTAM BOOKS
NEW YORK • TORONTO • LONDON • SYDNEY • AUCKLAND

RL 4, age 10 and up

REVENGE OF THE RUSSIAN GHOST
A Bantam Book / March 1990

CHOOSE YOUR OWN ADVENTURE® is a registered trademark of Bantam Books, a division of Bantam Doubleday Dell Publishing Group, Inc. Registered in U.S. Patent and Trademark Office and elsewhere.

Original conception of Edward Packard

Cover art by Romas Kukalis
Interior illustrations by Stephen Marchesi

ISBN 0-553-28381-2

Published simultaneously in the United States and Canada

Bantam Books are published by Bantam Books, a division of Bantam Doubleday Dell Publishing Group, Inc. Its trademark, consisting of the words "Bantam Books" and the portrayal of a rooster, is Registered in U.S. Patent and Trademark Office and in other countries. Marca Registrada. Bantam Books, 666 Fifth Avenue, New York, New York 10103.

PRINTED IN THE UNITED STATES OF AMERICA

OPM   0 9 8 7 6 5 4 3 2 1

REVENGE OF THE
RUSSIAN GHOST

WARNING!!!

Do not read this book straight through from beginning to end. These pages contain many different adventures that you may have as an exchange student living in Russia. From time to time as you read along, you will be asked to make a choice. Your choice may lead to success or disaster!

The adventures you have are the results of your choices. You are responsible because you choose! After you make a choice, follow the instructions to see what happens to you next.

Think carefully before you make a decision. The world of modern Russia can be exciting, but Russia at the turn of the century could be dangerous. You might find yourself back in time, face-to-face with Rasputin himself!

Good luck!

It has been dark and gloomy all day in Leningrad, the former capital of the Russian Empire. You're hurrying along the River Neva to the Nevsky Prospekt, the largest avenue of Leningrad, on your way to meet your friend Ilya. She has promised you a surprise for tonight. The evening will start at one of the famous old restaurants of Leningrad, the Metropol.

You never expected to end up in Russia when you arranged to do an internship for a semester at the Institute for Alternative Medicine. But you got along so well with the research team that they asked you to come along with them on a trip to the Soviet Union to study Russian folk medicine and traditional healing.

Your team is part of an exchange program with a group of Soviet students studying similar practices. After you're done in Russia, they will come to the United States to study holistic medicine in America.

Turn to page 2.

So far, the program has been fascinating. The Russians have told you what they've learned about folk remedies, herbal medicine, and faith healing. And you've brought them up-to-date on what you have learned about the connection between mind and body—how the mind seems to have much more of an influence over what happens in the body than was previously thought.

You've also gotten to know a member of the Soviet team, a Russian girl your age named Ilya. Over the past week you've become fast friends.

You've been surprised at how much the two of you have in common, though she does retain certain distinctly Russian traits. She's one of the new breed of Russians—someone who is not afraid to speak her mind and who is interested in learning about the West. She wants to hear all about the latest music, movies, and fashions in America. Meanwhile, from her you are learning about the Soviet Union, a country that has been closed to Westerners in many ways ever since the revolution in 1917.

As you walk along the Nevsky Prospekt to your meeting with Ilya, the air in the city seems to be thickening. It's not quite dusk, but already the streetlights are on. The whole day has been like this. It didn't really get light out until about ten this morning. There's been a heaviness in the air, and a burning smell. The city seems to be brooding.

Ilya has promised a special evening. She wouldn't say what it was, she just told you to meet her at the restaurant.

Go on to the next page.

You arrive at the Metropol and find Ilya waiting in line. She greets you in the Russian way, with three kisses on the cheek. "There's only a half-hour wait," she tells you cheerily.

"Not bad—for this country," you reply. "As far as I can tell, waiting in line is a national pastime here in Russia."

"Very funny," Ilya says. You like to tease her about the shortcomings of her society.

Forty-five minutes later you're seated at a table inside the Metropol. A waiter brings a menu, apologizing that only one is available. You've learned enough Russian to get by, so you don't need to ask Ilya to translate it for you. "Let's splurge," Ilya says, "and get caviar."

"Yuck," you reply. "You won't catch me eating those little fish eggs."

"Come on," Ilya says. "You have to at least try it. You won't truly have experienced Russia if you don't."

The waiter returns, and you give your order. He shakes his head impatiently and says, "Out." You try again and have to go through half the menu before you find a dish that's available. Ilya orders her caviar.

Turn to page 10.

You walk stiffly in your frozen clothes. The policeman introduces himself as Boris.

You're glad when you get to the warmth of the police station, but the sergeant in charge is not as cordial as Boris. He books you brusquely and then demands, "What's in the box?"

You'd forgotten you still had the shoe box under your arm. It feels like it's become part of your body. "I don't know," you say.

The sergeant narrows his eyes at you. "Open it up," he directs Boris. "Maybe you are a terrorist in disguise. You have a bomb in there, perhaps?"

You watch with dread as Boris removes the lid. "It's just an old boot," he shrugs, showing the sergeant the open box. Boris hands it back to you, and sure enough, inside is a beat-up old leather boot. It's several sizes too large for you.

"What do you want that for?" the sergeant demands with irritation.

"You never know when you might need it," you reply. But you're as mystified as he is.

Turn to page 33.

At the KGB station you and Ilya are taken into separate rooms. An agent begins to interrogate you.

"Why did you throw the box in the river?" he says.

"Because it was hot," you answer.

"You mean *stolen*? Don't use your American slang with me."

"No, no," you say hastily. "It was burning my hands." You go on to explain how you met the man with the box at Madame Kolodnia's and how he thrust it into your hands as the séance went up in flames.

After you've finished, the agent just looks at you. You know your story sounds outlandish. "I swear that's what happened," you add. "What was in the box, anyway?"

"An historical artifact," he snaps. "You were going to smuggle it out of the country, were you not?"

"No!" you exclaim.

Turn to page 67.

You and Ilya bundle up and leave the restaurant, walking into the cold Leningrad night. As you make your way through the swirling snow, you feel more and more apprehensive about what you're getting into.

You turn off the busy thoroughfares and go down crooked side streets into a neighborhood of grim, dilapidated buildings. The wind whistles through the tiny spaces between the buildings, and the streets are deserted. You and Ilya walk in silence.

As you approach the door to Madame Kolodina's flat, a man suddenly emerges from the shadows. "A moment of your time," he asks.

The sound of his voice makes you jump. You grab Ilya's arm, and she rings the doorbell.

"I don't like this," you say to Ilya. "Forget about the séance. Let's get out of here."

"Don't worry," Ilya says. She rings the bell again, but no one comes.

"I want to talk to you," the man rasps. He's wearing a dark overcoat and holding a shoe box under his arm. He starts toward you.

If you grab Ilya's arm and run, turn to page 89.

If you remain at the door and tell the man to go away, turn to page 24.

The conditions in the shelter are horrible, but you meet all kinds of people there. Besides the many down-and-outs like yourself, there are starving artists, writers, and actors. There is a whole crew of scribes who earn a pittance by copying plays for the theater.

In your old life you were handy at sewing, and so you fall in with a group known as the "tailors." They're in league with a gang of thieves who steal fur coats. The tailors take the coats apart, turning them into hats, boots, and gloves that their original owners will never recognize. This provides you with a job of sorts, or at least enough money to keep a spot on one of the hard benches at the shelter. When the revolution comes, you're quite ready to help throw the czar and the rest of the upper classes out of power.

The End

You look up to see a policeman coming down the bank toward you. But he's like no policeman you've ever seen. He wears elaborate ornamentation and an old-fashioned overcoat. He's big and hearty and has a huge handlebar mustache.

"Come on," he says in a jovial voice. "I'll help you up. We'd better get you down to the station and thaw you out."

Teeth chattering, you nod mutely. The policeman helps you climb the embankment, and as you reach the top, you notice you're not hearing the sounds of the city you expect to. Instead of the steady roar of traffic along the boulevard, you hear the jingle of sleigh bells, the rattling of trolleys, and the occasional putt-putt of an automobile.

"Where are we?" you ask the policeman.

"It was that bad last night, eh?" the policeman jokes. "Welcome to Petrograd."

Petrograd! That was the name given to Saint Petersburg just before the 1917 revolution, before it was renamed Leningrad in 1924. You're in pre-revolutionary Russia!

Turn to page 35.

By the time the food comes, you're ravenous. You start eating and ask Ilya, "So what's the surprise?"

"Close your eyes and open your mouth," she says.

Without thinking, you comply. She puts something in your mouth, and you chomp down. It's cold, with lots of little juicy balls, and slightly fishy. "Caviar!" you choke out, your eyes bulging.

"It's good, isn't it?" Ilya says, smiling. "But that's not the surprise."

"All right," you say to Ilya sourly, forcing yourself to swallow the caviar. "What's the real surprise?"

"The real surprise is that we're going to a séance tonight," Ilya answers.

"A séance? You mean like with Ouija boards, crystal balls, talking spirits, and all that?"

"Exactly," Ilya says. "But without the Ouija boards. You should take this seriously—I thought you wanted to learn about Russian mysticism?"

You sigh. "I do. It's just that it's been such a strange day. Everything has been so dark and gloomy, with that weird burning smell in the air. I feel spooked."

"Now you're starting to see the real Leningrad," Ilya says, not smiling. "Tonight will be very special. The séance is being conducted by Madame Kolodnia. She's recently arrived from Siberia, and her powers are supposed to be very great. I've heard she even has some gypsy blood in her. Tonight she will try to contact the spirit of Rasputin."

Turn to page 19.

12

Tatyana is a withered old woman with sparkling black eyes. She looks you over and decides to permit you to enter her wagon.

You put the shoe box up on the table, open it, and ask her what it's all about. She lifts the boot out of the box and handles it for only a few seconds before a look of distaste comes over her face and she drops it.

"This is an insult!" she cries, wiping her hands. "Get it out of here! Get out!"

You pack up the box and exit quickly. You decide to find Paul and ask him what could have made Tatyana so upset. He goes to her wagon and a few minutes later returns with an explanation. "To be honest, it sounds like she was baffled by your boot. She was also disturbed, because she could feel it had very great force. But since she couldn't interpret it, she became angry. She realized it was beyond her powers."

"What can I do?" you ask.

Go on to the next page.

Paul thinks for a moment, then says, "You could go to Maria. Everyone speaks of her powers." He lowers his voice and says reverently, "She is a witch."

"Where can I find Maria?" you ask.

Paul shrugs. "Gypsies have no address. But I think she is in the south, in the Azerbaijan region. It is a long way away. You would just have to ask when you got there."

You wonder if it's worth making the journey. Should you set off in search of Maria or stay with Paul's caravan?

If you decide to try to find Maria,
turn to page 96.

If you tell Paul you want to stay with him and
his caravan, turn to page 38.

You and Ilya take this opportunity to slip away from the man with the shoe box. You go into another room, where a long oval table is set up for the séance. You sit as far away from the man as possible.

Madame Kolodnia enters and sits at the head of the table. Her hair is bright red, and shining gold loops dangle from her ears. She takes a moment to fix everyone at the table with her dark, penetrating eyes and then says, "Tonight is a very special night. We will attempt to contact the spirit of Grigory Yfimovich Rasputin, the famous holy man." Nodding at you, she says, "We have a guest joining us who has come all the way from America to learn about Rasputin's healing powers."

You blush and nudge Ilya, who just shrugs. Madame Kolodnia asks the group to join hands and close their eyes. She begins the séance, calling up the spirit of Rasputin. For a long time nothing happens. People begin to shift in their chairs and let out little coughs. The room seems hot.

"Patience," Madame Kolodnia whispers. "He will come."

Slowly you become aware that the walls are trembling, at first only slightly, and then with increasing force.

Turn to page 30.

The party really gets going when the gypsies get out their guitars and the best singer in the camp stands up to do some heartrending gypsy songs. As she sings, Rasputin breaks into tears and starts philosophizing to the group gathered inside the tent.

"The gypsies are the only ones who understand the true sadness of life," he says, waving his glass around. "Listen to her voice. There is nothing like it in the world. With her voice, in the deepest laments she finds joy."

You listen to the songs and, like everyone else in the tent, start to become hypnotized. But the spell is broken by the sounds of hoofbeats and gunfire outside. You run out to see what is happening.

A gang of rowdy cossacks is galloping through the camp on horseback, firing their guns into the air. The cossacks are professional soldiers who have long been an elite cavalry corps in Russia.

The cossacks gather outside the tent, and the captain loudly demands to see the leader of the gypsies.

When the gypsy chief appears, the cossack captain proclaims, "We are on our way to the western front to fight the Germans, and we desire a last night of revelry. You will provide us with food and drink and entertainment, at once!"

With that, he dismounts and strides into the tent, his saber rattling and pistol smoking.

Turn to page 34.

"Don't look so unhappy," Rasputin says, his bright blue eyes once again sparkling. "It is my problem, not yours. This is not the first premonition I have had of my death. This only confirms it."

He claps his hands together and continues, "But you do have a problem, and that is how to get back to the world you came from. And I think I know how to solve that."

Rasputin pulls up a chair and sits directly across from you. "Look straight into my eyes," he says. "Do not take your gaze away from them. Concentrate on what I am saying. Think of nothing else."

You stare into Rasputin's intense blue eyes, and soon you feel as if you are falling into them, falling into bright blue pools of water. . . .

Turn to page 52.

18

As you flee through the crooked streets of the neighborhood, you're aware of dark shapes following you. You can't make out who or what they are, but you don't stop to try. Your legs just keep pumping as fast as they can.

Suddenly you come out into a large space. It's a wide, deserted boulevard. On the other side is a bridge. You cross the boulevard and stop to read a placard on the bridge's entrance—PETROVSKY BRIDGE. You're at the River Neva.

A hand on your shoulder nearly makes you jump out of your skin. "Ilya!" you cry when you see who it is.

She grabs your hand and starts running across the bridge. "This way!" she says breathlessly.

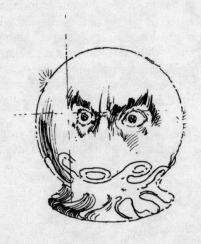

Turn to page 31.

"Rasputin!" you exclaim. "I thought he was a horrible monster."

"He was, in some ways," Ilya responds. "But he was also reputed to have great healing powers. He became the personal adviser to the czar and czarina, Nicholas II and Alexandra. Several times they credited him with saving their son's life, and once he supposedly raised another relative of theirs from the dead."

"I guess I don't know that much about him, other than that he was a monk of some kind."

"He was mostly self-taught," Ilya says. "Some say he was a holy man, others said he was a devil. He was born a peasant in Siberia, and through luck and his personal magnetism, he became the most powerful man in Russia next to the czar.

"Many of the aristocracy were scandalized by this and wanted to get rid of him. Finally a prince took things into his own hands and, after many attempts, suceeded in assassinating Rasputin." Ilya leans over and goes on in a low voice, "He was killed on this very night—December sixteenth. That's why this séance will be so interesting."

You shiver. "I'm not sure I want to go."

"Come on," Ilya says, picking up her coat. "Whatever you think of all this, it'll be a fascinating experiment."

Turn to page 7.

As you expected, when you come to the surface, you're near the bank of the river. Ilya is waiting for you, and she helps pull you out of the water.

Once you get back to her apartment and recover from the cold, you explain to Ilya what happened. "The man at the séance was trying to sell us a relic from 1916—Rasputin's boot. It came off after he was murdered and before his assassins threw his body into the Neva.

"When Madame Kolodnia called up Rasputin's spirit at the séance, it went mad with rage because of the presence of the boot—because it was being sold to the highest bidder. When the man gave the boot to me, you and I were drawn to the spot on the bridge where Rasputin was thrown into the river. Somehow, when we jumped in with the shoe box, it took me back to the time when he was about to be murdered."

"So by returning his boot to him, you quieted Rasputin's spirit," Ilya says. "That means Madame Kolodnia should be able to safely conduct her séance now."

"Right," you say. "But I wonder what happened to the boot the man gave me?"

You go back to the riverbank and find the shoe box there. When you open it, it is empty.

The End

In one motion, you fling the shoe box over the side of the bridge, grab Ilya, and pull her back down onto the snowy sidewalk.

The police cars skid to a halt, but before the officers can get to you, the dark figures following you arrive. They turn out to be men in black overcoats and hats. One of them grabs you, and the other takes Ilya.

"You're under arrest for throwing a Russian national treasure into the Neva," says the man holding you.

"You mean that shoe box?" you ask.

"That's exactly what I mean," he says.

The other man waves the police away, saying, "Leave this to us. This is not a police matter." He commandeers one of the police cars, and as you're bundled inside, Ilya whispers to you, "Oh no. These guys are KGB."

Turn to page 5.

22

You take Ilya's hand, climb up onto the parapet, and fling yourself into the abysmal waters of the Neva.

You don't remember hitting the surface layer of ice and breaking through to the water. Instead, you experience a very pleasant, cool, soothing sensation. In some very removed part of your mind, you think you must be having an out-of-body experience. Maybe this is death, you think. If so, it's not so bad.

You open your eyes to find yourself alone on the bank of the river. Ilya is nowhere to be seen. Harsh gray light hits your eyes. You're shivering, shot through with cold. Your hair is frozen, and even your eyelashes are iced. The longer you're awake, the more the chill penetrates. It is painful, and you just want to go back to sleep.

Just then a booming voice comes from above. "Another vagrant, eh?"

Turn to page 9.

"Go away!" you tell the man at Madame Kolodnia's door. Ilya tries the knob and finds that it's unlocked. You both rush inside, shutting the door and locking it behind you.

You run up the stairs, kicking the snow off your boots. On the top floor is Madame Kolodnia's flat.

You enter a very strange world. The room is suffused with candlelight, coming from rows of candles all along the walls. Above the candles hang dark icon paintings, and next to them are weird objects you can't quite figure out. The smell of incense wafts through the air.

Even stranger than the objects in the room are the people. You've met some odd characters in the course of your work at the institute but none compared to this. In a glance you see a bald-headed woman, a man with a black beard dressed in colorful robes, and an olive-skinned gypsy, among others. Plus—the man who accosted you outside!

You draw a sharp breath. "How—" you begin. But the man approaches, still carrying the shoe box under his arm. He kisses Ilya three times on the cheek, saying, "Ilya, darling, how nice to see you."

Go on to the next page.

"Do you know him?" you ask Ilya.

"Now I remember his voice—he has called me several times on the telephone," Ilya says. She gives him a cold look. "But I don't know him. He claims he has something for you."

"Me?" you squeak.

"That's right," the man says in his low, raspy voice. "An object of great value, which I think you'll find of supreme interest. If you will allow me—"

But the man is interrupted by the tolling of the midnight bells. Someone claps their hands and announces, "Attention, please. It is time for the séance to begin. Everyone please sit down at the table."

Turn to page 15.

26

With a heave, you throw the tray of hot tea at the cossack captain's head. He screams and drops his pistol, putting his hands to his face. Chaos ensues as Rasputin takes charge and leads the gypsies in routing the cossacks from the tent and back to their horses. Helping their injured captain onto his horse, they quickly mount and flee.

Once the cossacks are gone, Rasputin claps you on the shoulder and says with a laugh, "That was a daring move you made back in the tent. I thought I was done for. You saved my life!" He seems to find the whole thing very amusing.

"Let the festivities resume!" he proclaims in a booming voice. He draws you back into the tent with him, making you his guest of honor for the night.

The party finally draws to a close as the sun comes up in the morning. Rasputin, who has fallen into a deep, snoring sleep, wakes up and tells his entourage it's time to return to Petrograd. Turning to you, he says, "If you ever need anything, come by my flat."

"Actually," you say, "there is something I would like to talk to you about—in private. Can I come back to Petrograd with you now?"

"Certainly," he says with a yawn. "You can ride with me."

Turn to page 85.

An officer comes to release the four of you, and as you walk down the corridor, you ask the gypsy if he can help you out.

"Of course, my friend," he answers, "but what kind of help do you need? I'm only a gypsy."

Embarrassed, you reply, "I have no place to sleep tonight, and very little money." Then you get an idea. "I can teach you about herbal medicine, if you'll take me in."

"It's a deal," he says. "What's your name?"

You tell him and then ask him his name. "My real name is a secret," he replies, "but you can call me Paul."

Outside the station you get on a tram for the long ride to the outskirts of Petrograd. Paul explains to you that the gypsies aren't allowed to stay within the city limits, so they set up their camps just outside.

Along the way, Paul tells you about gypsy life. You find out they're a people unto themselves and that according to legend their race dispersed many centuries ago to the ends of the earth. They continue to live a nomadic life, traveling and living in wagons and tents. They make a living as artisans, traders, musicians, dancers, and fortune-tellers.

You reflect that you'll probably learn more about herbal medicine from the gypsies than they will from you but still you may know some things from your research that they don't.

Turn to page 42.

The next day, Fyodor has a change of heart. He suddenly decides to help you get in to see Rasputin. "But don't go to his flat," Fyodor says. "If you really want to get his ear, you must catch him at Tsarskoye Selo, the imperial palace outside Petrograd. He goes there every morning to visit Czarina Alexandra. There he tells her how to instruct Czar Nicholas II to rule the country."

"But how will I get in there to see him?" you ask.

"It's very simple," Fyodor replies with a smile. "You sneak in. Don't worry, we have methods to help you. It won't be difficult."

"It sounds like it would be much easier just to get in line with the petitioners," you say, feeling doubtful.

Fyodor rolls his eyes and says, "That's for fools. Hundreds of people see Rasputin there every day, and he doesn't pay any real attention. If you want Rasputin to listen to you, you must find him at Tsarskoye Selo."

You're not sure what you should do.

If you decide to sneak into the czar's palace, turn to page 51.

If you decide to get in the petition line, turn to page 45.

The vibrations increase. Objects on the side tables start to rattle. A vase crashes to the floor. The pictures on the wall start to fall off, one by one, and the oval table begins to shake. Then, suddenly, several candles fall to the floor, igniting the curtains. A tremendously angry force is in the room, whipping through it like a hurricane.

There is panic at the table. People are shrieking, and everyone gets up at the same time to flee.

The guests are running into one another in a mad rush to leave. You trip over someone and fall headlong to the floor. You scramble to your feet, jostled by the crush of bodies around you. The flames from the curtains rise higher and higher. "Ilya!" you cry. But you can't find her.

Suddenly you're face-to-face with the man with the shoe box. "It's burning my hands!" he cries, and thrusts the shoe box at you. You take it without thinking, but don't feel any heat coming from it.

"Over here!" a woman calls. You turn around and rush to a window she's raised, which opens out onto a metal fire escape. You clamber out and climb down the fire escape as fast as you can. When it ends fifteen feet above the ground, you jump into a snowbank. You get to your feet and run as fast as you can away from the burning building.

Panic has seized you. Shapes are running every which way in the dark. You just keep running, without thinking. All you know is that you want to get as far away from that terrifying force in the room as you can.

Turn to page 18.

Looking back, you see the dark shapes are still following you. Halfway across the bridge, coming from the other direction, are flashing lights—it's the police.

Ilya leads you to the side of the bridge. "We must escape," she says, her breath coming in short gasps. Her face is ghostly white.

She starts to climb up on the parapet of the bridge. You grab her, saying, "Ilya, no!"

"You don't understand," she hisses urgently. "We must escape." Her eyes are glazed.

"It's too dangerous," you say. But she's on top of the parapet. She starts pulling you after her. "Come on," she insists. "It's our only choice."

Suddenly you feel heat in your hands—you realize that the shoe box is now very hot. The police are closing in from one side; the shapes pursuing you from the other.

Ilya seems to be in a trance, but maybe she knows what she's doing. You feel a strange pull, too, as if icy fingers are drawing you into the river. Maybe you should jump with her.

Then again, maybe the shoe box is the cause of all the trouble. Perhaps you should throw it over the edge instead, and be rid of it.

If you climb up onto the parapet with Ilya, turn to page 22.

If you throw the shoe box over the side, turn to page 21.

The sergeant decides you're a loopy but harmless foreigner and allows Boris to take you to the holding tank so you can thaw out.

"Good luck, my friend," Boris says as he leaves you. "I hope life gets better for you."

You thank Boris and settle in with three other prisoners around a samovar in the middle of the room. The ice in your clothes slowly melts, and soon you are taking off your outer garments to wring the water out of them.

"What happened, did you fall in the river?" asks one of the prisoners, an olive-skinned man with ringlets of curly hair over his ears. There is a twinkle in his coal-black eyes.

"As a matter of fact, I did," you answer flatly.

"That can be bad for your health," he observes.

"Not as bad as the czar's police," the other prisoner comments. He's a thin man with a goatee, intense gray eyes, and rimless spectacles.

"And well they should be hard, Fyodor, with devils like you about," says the third prisoner from the corner, who is dressed in monk's robes.

The thin man named Fyodor glares at the monk in the corner. "It will not be long, Iliodor. The corrupt clergy, the greedy owners, and the incompetent ruling classes have all gotten fat off the toil of the masses. But the day is coming when the people will rise up and throw off their chains. Then you and your ilk will find out who the real devils are."

Turn to page 84.

You go into the kitchen tent to take a tray of hot tea to the guests. As you come back through the door of the main tent, you see the cossack captain, standing a few feet inside, faced off with Rasputin. The captain cuts a striking figure in his tight-waisted green tunic, baggy pants tucked inside his boots, and tall fur hat. Rasputin is equally striking as he rises from his seat and glowers at the cossacks.

Rasputin breaks the silence, "You are very rude, my friend. What right do you have to burst in here with your guns and swords? You're barbarians." Rasputin's voice builds to a shout. "You have no respect for the gypsies, and no appreciation of their music. Your ears are not worthy of it. Get out of here, right now!"

The captain draws himself up and spits words back at Rasputin. "How dare you speak to me like that, you animal? You're a disgrace to the czar, and a blight on holy Russia!"

Rasputin flings a glass at the captain in anger and orders, "Leave at once."

The captain's eyes narrow, his mouth sets, and he very deliberately pulls his pistol from his holster.

You are standing five feet from them, near the entrance to the tent, the tray of hot drinks in your hands. A hush comes over the tent as the cossack takes slow and deliberate aim at Rasputin.

If you throw the tray of hot drinks in the captain's face, turn to page 26.

If you decide you'd better remain still, turn to page 44.

As the policeman walks you to the station, you venture to ask him the year. He just laughs and says, "It's nearly the end of 1916, my friend. You must have had quite a night."

"Yes," you murmur, "I did."

"You speak strangely," the policeman adds. "Where are you from?"

Thinking quickly, you say, "I'm English." You know that many Britons and Europeans lived in Petrograd before the revolution.

"Ah, that explains it. Well, English or not, I'll have to book you for vagrancy. But don't worry. It'll give you a chance to warm up. It looks like you could use it."

The street is full of life. Women carry baskets on their heads, newsboys hawk their papers, kiosks and bazaars bustle with activity. But you get the same sense of foreboding as before. It's even stronger now—there's a frenzy to all the activity and a feeling of doom. The air is heavy and a purplish brown. And you smell that same burning odor from before.

Turn to page 4.

36

Sentries soon arrive, and you're hauled off to the police station in Petrograd. You're quickly brought before a magistrate. You plead innocence and tell your whole story, hoping that you'll be declared insane rather than guilty of attempting to assassinate the czarina. "Your story is preposterous," the magistrate says, "but I will think your case over and sentence you tomorrow."

That night you learn through the prison grapevine that Fyodor and his friend have been caught on the road back to Petrograd. The bomb plot is pinned on them, but the magistrate is still suspicious of you. The next morning, he sentences you to exile in Siberia. However, it's left up to you to get there.

Since you have no money, you end up destitute on the streets of Petrograd. You manage to survive by begging, which gets you enough money for a crust of bread and a spot on the floor in a night shelter.

Turn to page 8.

As your three companions in the holding cell continue their banter, you think about your predicament. You're in prerevolutionary Petrograd in the dead of winter. You don't know how you've gotten here or how to get back to Leningrad in your own time. You figure it must have something to do with the boot in the shoe box, which became strangely hot just before you jumped into the River Neva. It may also have something to do with Rasputin, since it seemed to be his spirit that destroyed the séance at Madame Kolodnia's house. But whether the boot and Rasputin have anything to do with one another, and how you can find out, is a mystery.

One thing you do know is that you don't want to go back out into the cold. With no money and no place to go, you'll quickly freeze. You need to ask one of your cell mates for help. All four of you are about to be released, but which one should you ask?

From listening to them, you gather that the gypsy is going to return to his caravan. He seems warmhearted, yet you wonder how much he can really help you. Fyodor seems like the kind of person who'd be willing to take you in. He's obviously intelligent, but single-minded. Iliodor, the monk, may be in the best position to help you, yet he's also the most unpleasant.

If you ask the gypsy for help, turn to page 28.

If you ask Fyodor, turn to page 41.

If you ask Iliodor, turn to page 62.

Paul nods sympathetically when you say you'd rather stay. "It's a long trip," he says. "It might be hard to find her, and even if you did, who knows if she would be able to help you."

You go to bed that night as mystified as ever about how you've ended up in a gypsy camp in prerevolutionary Russia.

At three o'clock, the camp is roused by a group of carousers who arrive in automobiles. They're an odd, motley crew of well-heeled aristocrats, scruffy-looking artists, and police agents. They're quite drunk and want to be entertained.

The cook fires are lit, the musical instruments are taken out, and the dancers awoken for the guests' enjoyment. You help out as best you can. A tent is cleared for the festivities. As you bring a steaming tray of food in, you see a striking figure at the center of the group, bellowing with laughter, a woman on each arm. He's tall and imposing, dressed in leather, fur, and silk. His hair and beard stick out all over, and his eyes are bright and wild.

Tatyana grabs your sleeve, points to him, and hisses, "It's Rasputin! That boot you brought me has something to do with him, I can feel it."

Turn to page 16.

You're beginning to feel uncomfortable with the dinner conversation, even though you don't know who it is Prince Yussupov and his friends are planning to kill. They're certainly making no effort to hide their plot.

Then Iliodor suddenly stands up and announces, "Thank you for the meal, Prince, but we must leave now." Turning to you, he says, "I am making a pilgrimage to the Verkhoturye monastery in Siberia. You may come as my assistant. I know of a starets—a master teacher—there whom you can consult about your problem."

So, you realize, Iliodor did hear you before after all. But you're not the least bit sure you want to go to Siberia with him. Aside from the fact that his nonstop talk may drive you crazy, it's a long way away from Rasputin, Petrograd, and the River Neva.

Yet your only other option at the moment is to ask Prince Yussupov if you can stay on with him. Considering how much he likes Iliodor, you assume he'd be willing to have you. But do you want to be guest to a host who's in the middle of an assassination plot?

*If you decide to go with Iliodor,
turn to page 63.*

*If you ask Yussupov if you can stay at his
palace, turn to page 76.*

The guards come to release the four of you. As you leave the police station, you explain to Fyodor that you have no place to go and ask if he can help you.

"Of course, my friend," he replies, his breath forming clouds in the cold air. "Our door is always open to those without a home. As long as you don't mind dodging government agents."

Fyodor takes you back to his hideout in an industrial suburb of Petrograd. He introduces you to his wife, Elena, and then immediately forgets you as he goes about the business of planning the revolution.

After a couple of days of being shown around the district by Elena, you begin to see why Fyodor is so involved in his plans. The workers labor for twelve or fourteen hours a day, six days a week, in squalid, sooty mills, factories, foundries, and workshops. At night they sleep in gray buildings next door to the factories, which are little more than huge warehouses of workers and their families. Inside, the dormitories are crowded and dirty. They look more like stables than human living quarters. Some workers have to sleep right in the factories, among the machines and waste products of the shop.

Turn to page 53.

You're welcomed into the gypsy camp and immediately fascinated by what you see. It's bustling with activity, as women work over cook fires, men work at their crafts or sit around the fires smoking their pipes, and children run everywhere.

The women are dressed in many layers of brightly colored skirts, scarves, and blouses and adorned with all kinds of rings and necklaces. The men, too, wear bright colors, as well as shiny buttons. Much of the clothing looks patched together from a variety of materials.

The insides of the tents and wagons, while furnished very modestly, are well kept and clean. Tables, chests, trunks, beds, quilts, food supplies, and tools are all neatly arranged in the small spaces.

You spend a couple of days helping out at the camp and discussing herb remedies and medicine with the gypsy women. You become accepted in the camp, and one day you venture to ask Paul if there is a fortune-teller who might be able to help you.

"Certainly," he says. "I will take you to see Tatyana. You would like to know your future?"

"Not exactly," you say. "I have a strange object, which may be supernatural."

"Ah, I see," Paul says, and tactfully asks no further. "Come with me."

Turn to page 12.

You hold your tray and watch helplessly as the cossack captain squeezes the trigger.

The tent explodes with the shot. Rasputin falls backward. The gypsies rush the cossacks, who beat a quick retreat to their horses and ride away.

Rasputin is bleeding heavily from the shoulder. The gypsies want him to stay, but his servants ward them off, carry Rasputin back to his car, and drive off.

You don't know how serious Rasputin's wound is or if you'll ever get a chance to talk to him. You stay at the gypsy camp, trying to figure out a way to pay him a visit. But a few days later, Paul tells you that Rasputin has mysteriously disappeared.

Soon Paul and his caravan pull up stakes and leave Petrograd. With nowhere else to go, you stay with them. They adopt you as one of their own. You like life with the gypsies, but you wonder if you'll ever figure out what the boot means and if you'll ever be able to get back to your own time.

The End

"I'm going to try the petition method first," you tell Fyodor. "If that doesn't work, I'll sneak into the czar's palace."

Fyodor flies into a rage. "Never mind!" he yells. "Go do it your own way—but don't ever come back to this house again, you ignoramus!"

You can't understand why he's so mad, but you stay out of sight for the rest of the day. Early the next morning, you get Rasputin's address from Elena. She secretly packs you a big lunch, a blanket for the cold, and some money for the trolley. "Good luck," she says. "And don't worry about what Fyodor says, if you need help you can always come back."

You thank her and set off for Rasputin's flat. After several trolley car rides, you find Gorokhovaya Street. The neighborhood is modest looking, as Elena said.

Rasputin's block is not hard to locate. It's the one with the line going all the way around it. You take your place in line and prepare for a long wait. Rasputin doesn't start to receive visitors until after noon.

Turn to page 73.

When you've finished your story, the starets sits deep in thought for a long time. Then he leaves without saying a word. He's gone for two days. You keep checking his cell, but when he is ready, he comes and finds you.

The first thing he says is, "I believe I understand where you come from, and I want nothing more to do with you. I especially want nothing more to do with that . . . thing," he says, pointing at the shoe box, which you still have by your side. "The smell of death and rot is all over it."

He pauses, having gotten that off his chest. "Now, I can help you to return to where you came from. All I ask is that you take that thing with you."

You agree immediately. You don't dare ask him further about the boot, since he obviously doesn't want to talk about it.

"What do I do?" you ask.

"Sit still, and promise you will leave me alone," the starets responds. Then he lights candles and incense, begins to utter strange incantations, and does all sorts of shamanistic things you wouldn't think a normal monk would know about.

But they work, and the next thing you know, you're back in Leningrad, washed up on the banks of the River Neva. Ilya looks at you questioningly, but you're no wiser than when you left. One thing you know is that you'll avoid séances at Madame Kolodnia's from now on.

The End

You stand your ground. "I will not leave," you say to Rasputin, "until you tell me what frightens you so about this shoe box."

Rasputin plops back into his chair, shaking, his eyes still ablaze. You tense your muscles, afraid he's about to do something really violent. But instead he puts his face in his hands, takes a deep breath, and orders you to close the door behind you.

"You are right," he says, looking up. "This box frightens me to the core of my being. You see, this boot—" He begins to break down again but recovers. "This boot is mine, and it foretells my death."

Sadness overcomes you as you see how frail and human Rasputin actually is. "But how?" you ask.

"I cannot explain," he says. "But you are from another place, another time, are you not?"

You nod.

"So is the boot—it is from after my death. I have had premonitions that my time is coming soon, but like all human beings, I preferred not to face the idea. By bringing this boot in, you have made me face it."

"I'm sorry," you say, earnestly.

Turn to page 71.

Quaking with terror, you grab the shoe box and run out the door of Rasputin's flat. You run down the steps two at a time and don't stop until you're well down the block.

Once you recover your wits, you're not sure what to do next. You have just enough money to take the trolley back to Fyodor and Elena's house, and you hope they will take you in again.

You knock at their door long after darkness has fallen. There is no answer. You knock again and then notice that the door is padlocked from the outside. That must mean that Fyodor and Elena have had to move to another hideout. With a chill of insight, you realize there is no one you can call and nowhere for you to go.

You manage to find shelter for the night in a nearby fiber factory, provided you start work the next day. You know it will be miserable, but at least you won't freeze to death.

It is only a week before you catch a cold, which turns into pneumonia, complicated by acute bronchitis. The medical care provided by the factory is next to useless. You don't even live long enough to see the revolution.

The End

50

Pretending to be converted by Yussupov's arguments against Rasputin, you say, "It sounds like you're planning a patriotic act. Is there some way I can help?"

Yussupov thinks for a moment and then says, "You may very well be able to help. Stay here in the palace, and I'll let you know when we need you."

Over the next few days, you sit in on Yussupov's meetings to plot the assassination. He and his associates decide to invite Rasputin over at midnight on the chosen night and tell him that Yussupov's wife, Irina, wants to meet with him. Yussupov will take him into a room in the basement specially furnished for the occasion and entertain him until Irina arrives. But Irina will never arrive, because Yussupov will give Rasputin a poisoned glass of wine to drink.

"This is where you come in," Yussupov says to you. "You will bring the wineglasses downstairs from the kitchen. Since you are the youngest, he will not suspect you of bringing him poisoned wine."

You nod mutely, trying to think of a way you can foil this plot.

Turn to page 87.

Fyodor sounds so sure of himself you decide he must be right. "If you can tell me where to go, I'll try to find Rasputin at the czar's palace," you say.

Fyodor claps his hands together. "Excellent," he says crisply, and you immediately begin plotting with him how to sneak into Tsarskoye Selo. Not only do you memorize the layout of the imperial grounds, you also get a quick lesson in the techniques of breaking and entering. "You don't have to break into the palace itself," Fyodor says. "Rasputin and Alexandra meet at her friend Anna Vyrubova's house so as not to attract the attention of the court. Anna has a small mansion—comparatively speaking—tucked away on the grounds."

The next morning you and Fyodor set out for Tsarskoye Selo, twenty-five kilometers outside of Petrograd. A friend of Fyodor's is driving, and he takes you around the back side, where you park in the woods a few hundred meters from the outer fence. Fyodor sends the two of you on ahead toward the fence while he makes up a rucksack for you containing a map and tools for climbing over fences and opening doors. "Don't forget the shoe box," you tell him.

"Don't worry," Fyodor replies.

Turn to page 65.

When you open your eyes, you are soaking wet and gasping for breath on the banks of the River Neva. Ilya is beside you, looking at you with a big question mark on her face.

"You're never going to believe this," you say to her as you begin your story.

She has a hard time believing it, but you're not surprised. You hardly believe your own story yourself.

The End

When you have a chance, you tell Fyodor you're curious to know where Lenin is. You're surprised to see a look of disgust come over Fyodor's face. "Lenin is nothing but a bookworm. He's cowering in Switzerland, hiding out in the library. He says we will never see the revolution in our lifetime. But the revolution will go on without him."

You refrain from telling Fyodor what you know—that in a few years the city he's in will be renamed Leningrad.

Meanwhile, you wonder how to get back to the Leningrad of your time. You ask Fyodor about Rasputin, but he dismisses him as a fraud. Elena, however, isn't so sure.

"One thing I know, Rasputin is very popular with the peasants," she says. "They come from far and wide to see him."

"You mean you can actually get in to see Rasputin?" you ask.

"Surprising, isn't it? He's probably the most powerful man in Russia right now, considering what a clod the czar is. Yet all you have to do to see him is get in line with your petition. People come to him with every kind of problem. Some want to be healed, some want to be granted an exemption from a law, some need money, and some just want his spiritual blessing."

"Where does he receive these petitions?"

"At his flat," Elena says. "He lives in a very modest place, right in the city."

Turn to page 61.

When you're done, Madame Kolodnia leans her forehead against her fingers, closes her eyes, and thinks for a while. Then she says, "First of all, that was no ghost that visited you last night. It was someone's idea of what a ghost should look like. Whoever it was was obviously trying to scare you. Who, or why, I cannot say.

"Secondly," she goes on, "our séance last night was not successful. We were unable to reach Rasputin. I sensed some blockage in the flow of his spirit. I can't say why, but I have a feeling it has some connection with your ghost."

"Maybe the police are behind it," you say. "It was strange that they arrived so quickly."

"That's true," Madame Kolodnia says. "They're never there when you need them, only when they need you. And they were obviously looking for something in Ilya's apartment."

"But why would the police—" Ilya begins.

"Wait a minute," you say, snapping your fingers. "The box—remember, the man last night had a box under his arm. It was a shoe box. And the Rasputin character was asking for his boot."

Go on to the next page.

"Yes," Ilya says, turning to you excitedly. "And now I remember—I recognized the man's voice. He's called me several times, trying to befriend me. He said he had an item of historical value that my American friend—*you*—might like to see."

"But," you muse, "a boot?"

"It sounds like the police know more about this than you do," Madame Kolodnia observes. "Perhaps you should ask them what's going on."

"Good idea," Ilya says. "We'll call them as soon as we get home."

You thank Madame Kolodnia for her help. "Let me know what you find out," she says. "It may help me to understand what went wrong at my séance."

Turn to page 106.

56

Finally, late in the afternoon, your turn comes. You're taken through the courtyard and up three flights of stairs to Rasputin's flat. The furniture is simple and practical, and the walls are decorated with icons and pictures of the czar and czarina.

Rasputin is seated at a table in the living room. His hair and beard are long and neatly combed. He wears a large cross around his neck and a long brown robe. But what nearly stops you dead in your tracks are his blue eyes. They seem to pierce right through you.

He snaps his fingers for your petition. Unsure what to do, you hand him the shoe box.

Rasputin impatiently opens the box. A look of shock and disbelief comes over his face as he contemplates the boot inside. For a moment, he seems to be at a loss—you have an odd feeling that you've knocked him off his guard. Then he turns his blazing eyes on you and begins to rage. "This is an abomination!" he screams. "How dare you present me with this, you devil! Get out, do you hear me? Get out right now!"

You cower in fright. Your urge is to do as he says and flee. But if you do that, you may give up your only chance to get help from him.

If you run out of the room, turn to page 49.

*If you stay and challenge Rasputin,
turn to page 47.*

Ilya shakes her head. "All this over a boot."

Katovsky returns with you to Ilya's apartment to wait for the phone to ring. Sure enough, the man with the shoe box calls again. You answer.

"This is the American?" he says. "Good. I have a business proposition for you."

"Ilya has told me of your calls. I'm ready to listen," you reply. "I'll remain at her apartment. Be here in an hour."

"You will not be sorry," the man says as he hangs up.

Turn to page 77.

You and Iliodor are shown into a dining room with a lavishly set table and a huge crystal chandelier hanging overhead. Several men are seated around the table, and Prince Yussupov, at the head, rises when he sees his new guests. "Iliodor, my old friend," he says warmly, "how delightful to see you. You are always welcome at my table."

Iliodor introduces you, and you sit down to a delicious meal. You try not to gobble your food, even though you're starving. You notice that Iliodor is quite uninhibited in this respect.

Yussupov is not exactly what you expected— he's young and dashing, perfectly coiffed, but somewhat of a dandy, given to extravagant gestures and coy mannerisms. Nevertheless, as you listen to the conversation, you soon realize that the subject under discussion at this elegantly appointed table is how to carry out an assassination!

"I say we just shoot him," one of the men says.

Yussupov wrinkles up his nose. "Too messy."

"Why not run him over with an automobile?" another man suggests.

"In public?" Yussupov says, seeming shocked. "Besides, it's not sure enough. I'm telling you, this man is stronger than a horse. He's superhuman. We must have a sure way of finishing him off."

The prince thinks for a moment. Soon a slow smile comes over his face. "Poison," he says wickedly. "It's secret, it's silent, and it's sure. I'll invite him over one night, slip a triple dose of poison into his wine, and the deed will be done."

Turn to page 40.

At that moment Fyodor walks into the room. You tell him your plan to visit Rasputin.

"Why?" he asks.

"I can't explain it all," you say. "Let's just say I have some questions for him."

"It's a waste of time," Fyodor says with contempt. "You'll spend all day in the cold on line. Then if you're lucky enough to get in to see Rasputin, he'll ask for your petition, ask for some money—or if you're a woman, he'll molest you—and make promises he has no intention of keeping. I guarantee you, at the end of the day, every one of those petitions will end up in the trash. He symbolizes everything that's corrupt in Russia."

"But Fyodor," Elena objects, "I've met people who have been helped by him."

"The man is a charlatan," Fyodor insists, settling the matter with a wave of his hand.

Turn to page 29.

"You seem like a very pious man," you say to Iliodor, knowing you need to flatter him. "Could I come with you when we get out of prison and study your ideas?"

Fyodor looks disgusted at your words. Iliodor inspects you with a severe eye. "I am a pilgrim," he declares. "My way is hard. You must be prepared to give up everything to follow me. I doubt you have what it takes."

"I'll do it, I'll give up everything," you insist. You neglect to mention that, at the moment, you have very little to give up. "I'm sure with such an excellent teacher as yourself, I'll soon be on the right path."

Iliodor, always looking for an audience, can't resist your reasoning. He agrees to let you become his student.

No sooner are you released from the holding cell than Iliodor starts a discourse about everything under the sun. "That man Fyodor made my blood boil," he says. "Those revolutionaries are the devil incarnate. They believe in nothing but themselves. Russia is in a bad enough state as it is without them going around setting off bombs. And we're in the middle of a war with Germany! Not that the czar knows the first thing about governing, but still he is the czar. I'm telling you, though, it's Czarina Alexandra who wears the pants in their palace."

As he talks, Iliodor leads you all over Petrograd, following no logic that you can see. You can't get a word in edgewise to ask where he's taking you.

Turn to page 97.

Thinking it's too risky to stay with Prince Yussupov, you say to Iliodor, "I'm ready to go."

He thanks the prince for the meal, and Yussupov says, "You're welcome, my dear Iliodor, and you know you can drop in whenever you like. Perhaps next time we will be discussing more pleasant matters."

The prince wishes you luck on your pilgrimage. Then you and Iliodor set off. It's a long and arduous journey, which takes you trudging through snow over the Ural mountains and sliding on sleigh over frozen Siberian rivers. You must rely on the kindness of strangers who take you in along the way, although Iliodor is famous enough that most people welcome you in. The hardest part of the journey is putting up with Iliodor's endless stream of opinion.

Finally you arrive at the Verkhoturye monastery, which you discover is near Pokrovskoye, Rasputin's native village. You and Iliodor are given small, bare cells to stay in. At your prompting, Iliodor promises that tomorrow he'll take you to see the starets he told you about.

Turn to page 102.

Soon the three of you are hidden behind a tree, timing the movements of the cossack horse patrols on the other side of the high iron fence. The cossacks, professional soldiers, wear red tunics, black fur caps, and boots. Sabers clank at their sides.

"There will be a break soon," Fyodor whispers. "Are you ready?"

You shoulder the rucksack. "I guess so," you say.

"Get to Anna Vyrubova's as fast as you can," Fyodor reminds you. "You don't want to miss Rasputin."

You sprint for the fence. You have only two minutes between patrols to climb over it, but the rope that Fyodor gave you helps you get to the other side quickly.

Turn to page 113.

In the middle of the night, you are wakened by a rattling noise. As you gradually gain consciousness, you realize that the door of the closet directly across from your couch is shaking. Then the windows start rattling, too. Maybe it's the wind, you think. Then a scratching sound comes from behind the wall.

You sit up, pulling the covers under your chin. Your ears are pricked now, listening for every noise. You think you hear a low grumbling somewhere in the room. The closet door rattles harder and harder, as if someone is trying to get out. A faint greenish light is leaking out from underneath it.

You're about to call out to Ilya when a low chuckle comes from the closet. It gradually builds to fiendish laughter.

You throw your covers off, run into Ilya's room, and shake her, but she won't wake up. She's as limp as a corpse. You feel her pulse, and it's barely there.

Turn to page 74.

The KGB agent turns around without saying another word and abruptly leaves the room.

You don't see him for another week, but when he comes back he tells you to get ready to go to the airport. "Amazingly enough," he says, "your story checked out. Luckily for you we were able to retrieve the artifact from the river and restore it to the rightful ownership of the Soviet people. We're going to let you off easy and deport you. But you must never come back here again."

This is not what you had in mind for your visit to Russia. But you have no choice but to comply.

The End

That night you're invited to dine informally in the prince's chambers. Yussupov is outfitted in a silk dressing gown and fur slippers. He leans back on a divan and eats from a tray. "So tell me," he says, popping a tart into his mouth, "have you been a follower of Iliodor's for very long?"

"Er, not too long," you reply.

"He is a good and pious man, though I must say he tends to run off at the mouth a little too much. What is this problem he was going to help you with?"

"It's spiritual in nature," you reply elusively. "I think it may have something to do with Rasputin."

"Rasputin!" the prince exclaims. "Now *there* is a starets. That man has colossal inner strength. He can see into the very soul of Russia. I have gone to him for treatment many times."

"What kind of treatment?" you ask nosily.

Yussupov throws his arms in the air. "Everything! It's not easy being a prince. We have had the most extraordinary hypnosis sessions. When I was under his spell, I'll tell you, I could feel his power," he says, clenching his fist.

"Maybe I should go see him then," you say.

"Oh no," Yussupov says, chewing madly and waving his hand. "You don't want to do that. I have come to realize that though he has phenomenal talents, Rasputin lacks judgment, temperance. He possesses power without responsibility, and there is no combination more dangerous. That is why he must die."

Turn to page 100.

You make some tea and sit up the rest of the night. In the morning, Ilya slowly wakens. "I feel like I've been asleep for a year," she says groggily. "My head is pounding."

"You should consider yourself lucky," you say, and proceed to tell her what happened while she slept.

She shakes her head in disbelief. "What the policemen did doesn't surprise me," she says. "But this apparition—the man you describe sounds like Rasputin!"

"Come to think of it, you're right," you say. "I've only seen a couple of pictures of Rasputin, but that's who he looked like."

"I guess your fears last night were well-founded," Ilya says. "But right now, the only person I know of who may be able to help us is Madame Kolodnia."

"Oh no," you say, as you remember how frightened you were last night at her doorstep. "I'm not going back there."

"But how do you know it was her fault?" Ilya insists. "She may be able to help clear this whole thing up for us."

You think again. Maybe Ilya is right. But then again, maybe you'll just get deeper into trouble if you go to Madame Kolodnia's.

If you decide to give Madame Kolodnia's another try, turn to page 111.

If you don't go back, turn to page 101.

Rasputin waves his hand. "It is not your fault. I must prepare for what is coming. But what about you—do you not want to go back to your own world?"

"Yes," you say. "That's why I came to see you. I had a feeling you might know what the boot—"

You stop short and then change the subject slightly, telling him about the séance and how his spirit wreaked havoc at Madame Kolodnia's. "Someone brought the boot to her house," you finish, "and that must have been what angered you."

Rasputin nods, looking thoughtful and still a little sad. But then he is all business. "I can help you get back to your time. You don't have to worry about my spirit disrupting your séances anymore. Where did you say you were when this happened?"

"Leningrad," you reply.

"Strange name for a city," he murmurs as he begins to put you into the trance that will return you there.

The End

After your meeting with Prince Yussupov is over, you say you're going to retire to your room. Before you go to bed, though, you ask one of the house servants for Rasputin's address. He gives it to you and helpfully tells you that if you mention Yussupov's name, Rasputin will give you an immediate audience.

You go to bed, but you're back up and dressed at four in the morning. You're careful as you slip through the halls of the palace toward an exit, but the few guards and servants who are awake don't pay much attention to you.

It's still pitch black outside as you start the long walk across the city to Rasputin's flat. At least by constantly moving you keep warm in the frigid Petrograd night.

You wait until the first rays of dawn, which come around nine o'clock to ring the bell of Rasputin's surprisingly modest flat. A housekeeper answers, and you tell her that Prince Yussupov sent you.

"The master is still asleep," she responds. "But I will tell him a friend of Yussupov's is here to visit."

The housekeeper gives you a seat in the living room and brings you some tea. A few minutes later, Rasputin appears, still in his nightclothes, rubbing his eyes and yawning. He apologizes, saying he had a hard night wrestling with demons.

"You come at the advice of my good friend Prince Yussupov?" he asks as the housekeeper sets a cup of tea and saucer before him. Even in his drowsy state, you can feel the force of his unusual powers and his intense blue eyes.

Turn to page 104.

As you stand in line, you hear stories of Rasputin's powers. A woman behind you says that he foretold her niece's marriage. Another woman says he cured her arthritis, and she's coming back for a second treatment. You also hear stories of his generosity. A well-to-do visitor will leave behind a pile of bribe money, which Rasputin will proceed to pass out to more needy visitors who follow, whether they're schoolgirls asking for tuition money or gamblers over their heads in debt.

Rasputin is obviously popular among the working people, country folk, peasants, and those down on their luck—at least the ones standing in line with you. Still, you remember Fyodor's warnings, and you keep on your guard. One thing Fyodor was right about, you do wait in line all day, shivering.

Turn to page 56.

74

Then the sound of splintering wood comes from the other room. You slowly edge back to the doorway and peer in. The moment you do, the closet door breaks off its hinges, and a huge bear of a man emerges. His hair and beard are matted and stick out wildly all over the place. His clothes are tattered and bloodstained. A weird greenish glow lights his face, and his eyes have a glazed look—he does not blink.

He takes halting, limping steps toward you and holds out his hand. "Give me back my boot," he intones over and over. "Give me back my boot."

You're terror stricken. But you have to do something.

If you say you'll give back the boot, turn to page 116.

If you tell the man you don't have his boot, turn to page 92.

You hesitate as Iliodor prepares to leave. "Maybe it's not such a good idea for me to go to Siberia," you say.

"You're certainly welcome to be my guest," Prince Yussupov suggests.

Iliodor looks hurt when you accept Yussupov's offer, but then he just shrugs and goes on his way. Yussupov directs a servant to make up a room for you.

Turn to page 68.

An hour later, the man knocks on the door. He is carrying the shoe box. You show him in, and he gets right to the point. "I have an artifact here that you can buy from me for next to nothing and sell for a great deal of money in America. There are many rich collectors there, are there not?"

"There are," you agree. "What's the artifact?"

You're not surprised when he repeats the whole story about Rasputin's boot. "All right," you say. "How much do you want for it?"

As soon as he quotes you a price, Katovsky bursts out of the closet where he's been hiding. He puts the man in handcuffs and informs him he's under arrest for attempting to sell an artifact belonging to the Soviet people.

The man looks at you with hate. "You set me up!" he accuses. "You could have become rich."

"That's all right," Katovsky says to you. "You'll be a hero and get a reward besides."

After Katovsky has taken the man away, you call Madame Kolodnia and tell her what happened.

"It's all beginning to make sense," she says. "By bringing the boot to my house, the man angered Rasputin's spirit. Now that the matter has been settled, we can conduct the séance with greater hope of success. I hope you and Ilya will come as my guests of honor."

The End

At three o'clock you're waiting on a bench in Lenin Park. The man shows up right on time. He's got the shoe box with him, and he's still wearing the same overcoat from last night. He sits down next to you and murmurs, "I'm very glad you came. I think this meeting will benefit both of us."

"Tell me what you want," you say impatiently.

"A small sum of money," he replies. "In return, I will give you a rare and exotic artifact."

"What's that?" you say skeptically.

He opens the shoe box. Inside is an old beat-up leather boot. "A most extraordinary bit of Russian history," the man says. "This is the boot Rasputin was wearing the night he was murdered. His assassins invited him over to their house for a midnight party. It took three tries—first with poison and then twice with pistols before they finally killed him. Rasputin was a powerful man with a powerful will to live. They took his body and dumped it in the River Neva, but on the way there one of his boots fell off. A fortunate set of circumstances has delivered the boot into my hands—and soon into yours."

"Why mine?" you ask.

"Because, my friend," he rasps, "I know you have an appreciation for such artifacts. It would be far too risky for me to sell this to a Russian. But you can take it back to America and sell it for many times more than you'll pay me."

Go on to the next page.

You consider the man's offer. At first you're sure it must be a fraud, but as you recall the strange events of last night, you begin to think that there may be something to it. Even so, do you want to get involved in something like this? Maybe you should turn him in to the police.

If you decide to make the man an offer, turn to page 112.

If you just pretend to be interested, turn to page 105.

Once the police leave, you get to work raising the money to buy Rasputin's boot. You go back to the hotel where your research team is staying and do some fervent salesmanship to get several other Americans to go in on the deal with you. It takes until midnight to raise all the cash you need.

The next day you meet the man in Lenin Park. You give him the money, and he turns over the shoe box with the boot inside. You decide to cut your visit to Russia short and head straight back to the United States with your purchase.

Everything goes smoothly until you get the boot back home. You go to collectors and museums all over the country, but no one will believe that what's inside the shoe box is actually Rasputin's boot. You tell them about the séance and the green ghost, but your story sounds more and more like fantasy, even to you.

With no way to verify the authenticity of the artifact, you're left with nothing but an old Russian boot and some very angry investors.

The End

"Come in," Maria says. You hand her the shoe box and take a seat on top of a trunk in her wagon. She inspects the boot very carefully, as if it is fragile, feeling every little fold in it. Then, with a shudder, she puts it down.

"This boot has death in it," she tells you. "You must leave it at once."

"But can't you tell me anything more about it? Who does it belong to?"

"It belonged to a very powerful man. But he was also reckless, and he has recently died. I do not know more than that. Really, my friend, I advise you to leave it at once."

"How can I get back to where I came from?" you ask with resignation.

Maria looks at your palm for a long time. "You must return to the River Neva," she says. "Prick your middle finger and let a drop of blood fall into the river, and then jump in. Go there at once."

You thank Maria and return to your caravan. You manage to scrape together the money you've earned over the past months to buy a horse. The next morning you sadly say good-bye to your caravan and set off for Petrograd.

When you arrive a month later at the Neva, you do as Maria has instructed. When you come to the surface of the water, you see Ilya standing on the bank, as if no time has passed. She calls you, and you manage to swim through the chunks of ice to the river's edge. You have an amazing adventure to tell her, but you still don't know how it all came about.

The End

"I pray that day does not come," Iliodor responds to Fyodor fervently. "It would mean the destruction of holy Russia."

"Yes," Fyodor says, "and the birth of a new Russia."

A sigh comes from the man with dark eyes. "Russia will always be Russia, and you two will always be at each other's throats."

"What do you know about it, you ignorant gypsy?" Iliodor spits. He doesn't seem to approve of anyone.

The gypsy shrugs and smiles. "I know what I know. Everything and nothing."

"What are you in for?" Fyodor asks him.

"Disturbing the peace," the gypsy replies.

"A noble cause," Iliodor mutters.

Fyodor ignores Iliodor's comment yet seems to agree with him. "Why do you waste so much energy on song and dance? I know you need to distract yourself from the misery all around you. But you could be using that energy to change the conditions of your lives."

The gypsy looks at Fyodor, his brow furrowed. "My friend, I can see you are a very dedicated man, with a righteous cause. But I fear you are too single-minded. If your revolution does not know how to dance, then it will be for nothing."

Turn to page 37.

Rasputin sleeps during most of the drive back to his flat. When you get there, his servants take him inside and make up a guest bed for you. They tell you not to disturb him until he's had a chance to rest up after last night's party.

Later in the day, as you wait in the living room of his flat, Rasputin emerges, bright and cheery. "Ah!" he says when he sees you, "you're still here. What can I do for you?"

"Please sit down," you say, handing him the shoe box, "and tell me if you know what this is."

"Whatever you say," he replies merrily. But his expression changes quickly when he looks inside the box. "You may have saved my life last night," he tells you, "but I feel something very ominous from this boot. It is a harbinger of my death."

You're taken aback. "But—" you sputter. "How can that be?"

Rasputin shakes his head slowly. "I can't say exactly. But I feel it right down to my bones. You see, this is *my* boot."

"How can it be that I have your boot?" you wonder.

"You—and this boot—are not of this world," Rasputin replies abruptly. "Is that not true?"

"Yes," you admit. "But isn't there some way I can help you prevent this from happening?"

"No, it is my fate," he says sadly. "I must accept it, and so must you."

You feel sad as well. Rasputin, despite all his faults, has not been the monster you had expected him to be.

Turn to page 17.

The appointed evening arrives, and one of Yussupov's accomplices, a doctor, sets off to bring Rasputin to the palace. You wait in the kitchen and a little while later hear the sound of friendly greetings and snow being clomped off boots at a back entrance.

The doctor bustles into the kitchen and prepares a tray with cakes, biscuits, and two glasses full of wine. His hands shake as he opens a vial of poison and drops it into one of the glasses.

"The tray is ready," he says to you. "Now remember, Yussupov's glass is next to the cakes, and Rasputin's is next to the biscuits."

You nod and pick up the tray. You descend the stairs to the basement slowly and carefully. As you enter the room where Rasputin and Yussupov are seated, you try to keep your own hands from shaking.

There's an uneasy silence in the room, as if the host and visitor don't know what to say to one another. "Some wine, perhaps?" Yussupov asks Rasputin.

Rasputin clears his throat and says, "Yes, why not?"

As you set the tray on a side table, you figure this is your last chance to head off disaster. You glance sideways and see that Yussupov has turned to look at a painting and is facing away from you. Should you switch the glasses?

If you switch the wineglass, turn to page 117.

If you decide it's too risky, turn to page 108.

You leave behind the heavy rucksack, tuck the shoe box under your arm, and race out of the woods as fast as you can for the nearest boundary of the palace grounds.

A cossack patrol quickly spots you and comes galloping after you, yelling, "Stop! You're under arrest!"

He never has a chance to arrest you all in one piece, because seconds later the bomb explodes in your hand.

The End

"Let's go," you whisper to Ilya. You grab her arm, and start running down the street.

"Wait!" the man calls after you, waving the shoe box. "I just want to talk!"

But you're convinced you must get out of there. You keep running, your hand clutching Ilya's coat, until you reach a main avenue. A taxi is coming by. You hail it, and once the two of you are safely inside, you give the driver Ilya's address.

"What's this all about?" Ilya demands angrily. "I wanted to attend the séance. Why did you make us run away?"

"I guess I just got a little spooked," you say. "I had a strange feeling to begin with, and then when that man came out of the shadows—"

Ilya sits with her arms folded the whole way home, giving you the silent treatment. Once you're back in the safety of her apartment, your fears start to seem silly. "Maybe I did overreact a little," you admit.

Ilya relents a little. "It was kind of creepy," she says. "Anyway, you can stay here tonight, on my couch. I'll get some sheets and blankets for you."

Turn to page 66.

The next day you arrive early in Lenin Park with Katovsky and his men. They hide in the bushes, and you wait on the bench for the man with Rasputin's boot.

He arrives at three o'clock on the dot, a big smile cracking his face. "Do you have the money?" he asks eagerly.

You shrug and say, "Not exactly."

The man's face falls. As he is about to speak, Katovsky's big paw falls on his shoulder from behind. "You're under arrest," Katovsky growls.

The man whirls and cries out in disbelief as he sees the police emerging from the bushes. Katovsky grabs the shoe box. "Take him away," he orders his men.

"You betrayed me!" the man cries at you. "You've blown your big chance. You could have been rich!"

You shrug and settle for having your picture in newspapers around the world the next day. You even get a reward from the Soviet government for the return of Rasputin's boot to public ownership. From here on in, the rest of your trip is a lot easier.

The End

"I don't have your boot," you say to the apparition with the huge green beard.

He keeps clomping toward you, growing angrier, his eyes bulging out, demanding, "I want my boot!"

"What boot?" you cry. "I don't know what you're talking about!"

"Murderer!" he screams.

You decide not to keep debating the point. You brandish a brass candlestick at the apparition. "Stop right there, or I'll clobber you," you threaten. "I'm calling the police."

The apparition stops and bursts into demonic laughter once again. You slowly back into Ilya's room, slam the door, and lock it. As you dial the police, the laughter in the other room grows louder.

"Help!" you cry when the police operator answers. "I'm being attacked by a huge green man!" You give Ilya's address, and the operator promises to send someone over right away.

As you hang up, you hear the front door slam. You cautiously peer into the living room. The apparition is gone.

The operator wasn't kidding—about thirty seconds later, two policemen knock at the door. You tell them a wild-looking green man was threatening you and saying something about wanting back his boot.

Go on to the next page.

"You have no idea who this man was?" one of the policemen asks.

"Never seen him before in my life," you answer. "Or his boot either."

The policeman just nods thoughtfully, and then without a word to you, he and his partner proceed to tear apart Ilya's apartment, searching it from top to bottom. All you can do is stand there, outraged and speechless.

When the policemen are done ransacking Ilya's apartment, one of them says, "We'll file a report at the station. Call us if you have any more trouble." He doesn't say a word about why they have just turned the apartment upside down.

Turn to page 70.

"What's going on here?" Boris demands.

"I'm telling you, they've murdered Rasputin!" you say.

Boris stops a passing car and orders the driver out. He jumps behind the wheel, and you get in the passenger seat. Together you go skidding after Yussupov's car on the snowy streets.

You finally catch up to them in the middle of the Petrovsky Bridge, where they've stopped. Yussupov and his men are carrying a large bundle toward the edge of the bridge. Boris yells at them to stop.

As you run toward them, you notice something familiar on the snow outside Yussupov's car. It's Rasputin's boot. It's an exact copy of the one in your shoe box!

Suddenly it all becomes clear to you. You pick up the boot and thrust it at Yussupov. "Here," you say, "you forgot his boot. You must bury it with him."

Yussupov, not understanding your motive, grabs the boot and says, "Good idea." He stuffs it inside the bundle containing Rasputin's body, and then his accomplices throw the body into the river.

Yussupov turns proudly to Boris and says, "Go tell your superiors that you have just witnessed a great event in Russian history."

You, however, are not worried about Russian history. You're climbing onto the parapet of the bridge, and before anyone can stop you, you dive back into the icy cold water of the River Neva.

Turn to page 20.

"I want to try to find Maria," you tell Paul.

"Very well," he says. "I think the best thing for you to do is wait for a caravan going to Azerbaijan."

You agree, and a week later Paul hooks you up with a gypsy caravan heading south. You thank him and say good-bye. "Good luck," he says, waving to you.

It is a long, hard trip to Azerbaijan, with many stops on the way. You see many amazing places as you travel, and you are astounded at the diversity of peoples who make up the Russian Empire, from the Latvians and Ukrainians in the west to the Uzbeks in the south. You'd never realized before what a vast land it is.

The end of summer has come before you finally get word from another caravan of where Maria is. You follow a trail of word-of-mouth until eventually you find someone who saw Maria last week and is able to tell you exactly where her caravan is. A few days later you are knocking on the door of her wagon.

The woman who opens the door is surprisingly young. She has raven hair and deep green eyes. You're dumbstruck for a moment, and then you stammer, "Maria?"

"I am Maria," she says.

You quickly explain that you have traveled for months to find her. You tell her your whole story, hoping she doesn't take you for a lunatic. "From what I have heard of your powers, you may be the only person who can help me," you finish.

Turn to page 82.

Iliodor goes on for a long time about how soft and decadent the imperial family have become, and how the country should return to the days of iron discipline. "And to top it all off, the czarina listens to no one but that holy devil!"

"Do you mean Rasputin?" you ask.

The mention of Rasputin's name really sets Iliodor off. He goes into a long rant about the mystic's crimes, some of which are truly harrowing. "He'll stop at nothing to get what he wants," Iliodor says. "I've heard that he has taken little children and chopped them up to use in his black magic potions."

Every once in a while you try to slip in a word to Iliodor. "I have a problem that may well be spiritual in nature, and I was wondering if you knew anybody who might be able to help me—" you start.

"It's not as if I haven't met the man," Iliodor goes on. "I knew him many years ago, before he became the fiend that he is today. He tried to recruit me, but I resisted temptation. No, he won't help anyone unless there's something in it for him."

"Maybe what I need is some sort of medium or mystic," you put in.

Instead of replying, Iliodor suddenly stops, takes you by the shoulders, and looks you straight in the face. "Are you hungry?" he asks.

"I guess so," you answer.

"Good," he says, starting off in a completely new direction. "I have a friend, a wealthy and cultured man, a prince, actually. He's a great patriot, and one of my biggest fans."

Turn to page 115.

Taking a few tools you may need to get into the house, you leave the ticking shoe box in the rucksack behind a tree. There isn't much time, so you just bolt for the rear of Anna Vyrubova's mansion. A garden trellis lets you climb up to a balcony, and from there you manage to pick the lock on a second-floor door. Soon you're prowling through the plushly carpeted hallways of the mansion.

As you pass a bathroom, you hear voices coming from downstairs. You find you're able to eavesdrop through an air vent. As you listen, you realize it's Rasputin, talking to the czarina! You can't believe you've managed to get so close to them.

Rasputin excuses himself, and a moment later you hear the heavy step of his boots on the stairs. As he enters the bathroom, you put your finger over your lips. "Shhh!" you say.

He jumps back with fright, ready to defend himself, but you immediately start explaining, in your lowest whisper, that you need to talk to him.

"Fine, fine," he whispers back, still trying to recover himself.

You start to tell him your story, but you don't get very far. A tremendous explosion from the woods outside blows out all the windows of the house. Rasputin grabs you in his big bear arms. You try to wriggle away, but you can't break his powerful grip.

"So you're up to no good after all," he says angrily.

Turn to page 36.

With a shock you realize it's Rasputin that the prince is planning to murder.

Seeing the recognition on your face, Yussupov goes on, "Yes, it is Rasputin we are going to kill. I regret it very much—I love the man. But I love Mother Russia even more than I do him. Even more than I love my own life. For the good of the nation, Rasputin must die."

"Isn't there a better way to get him out of the way?" you ask the prince, dazed.

"We've tried," he says grimly. "The czarina will listen to no one else. He can't be threatened or bribed. Any adviser who says a bad word about Rasputin is thrown out on his ear. No, this is the only course of action left."

Your mind is reeling. Should you let Yussupov and his friends go ahead with their plot? How will it affect your chances of getting back to Leningrad? What kind of danger are you in, now that he's revealed himself to you? you wonder.

You see two options. One is to pretend to help Yussupov and then double-cross him when you get the chance. The other is to try to slip out of the palace and warn Rasputin about the plot—although that may be just as dangerous.

If you pretend that you want to help Yussupov, turn to page 50.

If you decide to try to warn Rasputin, turn to page 72.

You fold your arms. "I'm not going back to Madame Kolodnia's," you say to Ilya. "I still have a bad feeling about it."

Ilya gives in. "All right, but what are we going to do?"

"I don't know," you admit. "We can start by cleaning up your apartment. The police sure made a mess of it."

While you're helping Ilya put her place back together, the phone rings. Ilya asks if you can get it.

You recognize the voice on the line immediately. It's the man who accosted you at Madame Kolodnia's last night. "I'm glad to be able to talk to my American friend personally," he rasps. "Why did you run away from me?"

"Because you're a creep," you answer.

"Creep I may be," he chuckles, "but I have a proposition for you. It's purely business."

"What's going on here?" you demand.

"I'll tell you everything," he promises. "And best of all, I'll tell you how I can make you rich. Meet me in Lenin Park at three o'clock this afternoon."

The line goes dead. You're looking at the phone as Ilya comes in. "Who was it?" she asks.

"That creep from last night," you say, and tell her about your conversation.

"Why don't you go and meet him?" she says. "You've got nothing to lose. There will be lots of people in Lenin Park, so it should be safe. Maybe then we'll get to the bottom of this."

Turn to page 79.

True to his word, Iliodor takes you first thing in the morning to the cell of the starets and then leaves. The starets is an old man with wrinkled skin and a long, scraggly beard. There's a kindness in his eyes but also a severity that makes you a little hesitant to spill your whole story. You decide to start by asking him if he knows anything about Rasputin.

"Rasputin!" he grunts, then smiles a little. "He came here when he was young. I tried to teach him, but it was impossible. He had no discipline. He would only follow his own way. It is no wonder he has strayed from the church. I am sorry for it. I'll tell you something, he had the spark in him. He could have been a very holy man. But instead— well, I guess he followed his own lights."

You're not sure what to do next, so you show the starets the shoe box. He looks at the box curiously and raises his eyebrows as he opens it. But no sooner does he pick up the boot than he lets it drop to the floor. He jumps back, making the sign of the cross and other gestures to ward off evil spirits. "Who are you?" he demands, his eyes alight with fear and anger.

Now that you're all the way out here in Siberia, with no idea where to go next, you take a deep breath and decide to just tell everything you know to the starets.

Turn to page 46.

"Yussupov is not your friend," you blurt out, and proceed to spill the whole story to Rasputin about the assassination plot.

Rasputin pours his tea out of his cup into the saucer and takes a few slow slurps. "Others have warned me of this," he says finally, giving a shrug. "I myself have sensed that my time is near. I do not know whether it will come at Yussupov's hand, or another's. But it is ordained. It is my destiny. If the result is my death, I must accept it."

Feeling that he has strong powers of understanding, you plunge in and explain your problem, starting with the séance in future Leningrad.

Rasputin seems unfazed by all this. "I will see what I can do for you," he says, slurping the last of his tea. "Lie down on the table."

You get up on the table and lie flat on your back. Rasputin stands and begins to hypnotize you, moving his hands above you. When he speaks, his voice seems to come from a great distance. You hear him say, "You can tell your friend that she may conduct her séance now. My spirit will not disturb it."

Your mind whirls, and soon you feel you are drifting into the rushing blue waters behind his eyes.

When you come to, Ilya is shaking you on the banks of the Neva. "We've got to get inside before we die of hypothermia," she says. "Where have you been?"

"It's a long story," you say. "You're never going to believe it."

The End

"Okay, I'm interested," you tell the man, trying to sound sincere. "How much do you want?"

He quotes you a figure, and you do a little haggling before finally agreeing on a price for Rasputin's boot.

"I'll bring the money here tomorrow," you say. "Same time, same place."

"Good," he says, breaking into a grin. "I knew you would appreciate my offer."

The police are waiting for you when you get back to Ilya's. "Where have you been?" a detective, who introduces himself as Katovsky, demands. "We know you received a call this morning. We suspect you of engaging in the illegal trade of Russian historical artifacts."

"You don't mean Rasputin's boot, do you?" you ask innocently.

"That's precisely what I mean," Katovsky replies.

"Don't worry," you tell the detective. "I've got it all set up. I'm meeting the man with the boot tomorrow at three o'clock in Lenin Park. You can grab him there."

"You better not try any tricks," Katovsky growls.

After the police leave, Ilya looks at you curiously. "Were you telling them the truth?" she asks.

"The whole truth," you say, and proceed to relate the events of your meeting to her.

"Weren't you a little tempted to buy it?" Ilya asks.

"Not really," you say. "It's not the kind of thing I'd want sitting around in my living room."

Turn to page 91.

You don't need to find two kopecks to call the police. A black KGB car is waiting for you outside Madame Kolodnia's house. A man opens the car door as you and Ilya approach. He motions for the two of you to get in. "We want to interview you," he says humorlessly.

Down at headquarters, the agent, whose name is Katovsky, takes you into an office and locks the door behind him. "What were you doing at Madame Kolodnia's?" he begins.

"Figuring out that your Rasputin ghost was a fake," you say boldly.

Katovsky flinches slightly, so you know you've hit the mark. "We don't have the boot you're looking for," you go on, "but we think we know who does. A man approached us last night with it." You go on to explain how you became frightened and ran away.

"If you are telling the truth," Katovsky says, "you will help us catch this man?"

"Gladly," you say. "But first tell me, what is this boot?"

Katovsky sighs. "It's a Russian historical treasure," he says. "A strange one, I admit, but valuable nonetheless. After Rasputin was assassinated in 1916 by a group of reactionary nobles, they threw his body into the River Neva. However, before he was thrown in, one of his boots came off. It's been on the black market ever since. This is the closest we've come to tracking it down. When we get it back, it will go into the Museum of the Great October Revolution."

Turn to page 58.

You leave the tray on the side table, bow to Prince Yussupov, and return to the kitchen. Your mind races, trying to think of how you can save Rasputin.

You sit with the other conspirators in the kitchen, waiting tensely for something to happen. You want to slip away, but you're afraid it would draw too much attention. Finally, an hour later, Yussupov comes running up the stairs.

"Nothing's happening," he hisses. "Did you put the poison in, Doctor?"

"A triple dose," the doctor answers. "Rasputin should be out cold by now."

"I tell you, he's superhuman," Yussupov says, clearly frightened. "He has some kind of evil power protecting him."

Yussupov runs back downstairs to attend to his guest. A half hour later, you hear him coming back up the stairs. You decide you have to do something—you'll go get the police. While everyone in the kitchen waits for Yussupov, you slip away. As you leave, you overhear him telling his friends, "He's still alive!"

Go on to the next page.

You're making your way toward a side exit from the palace when you hear gunshots. Shouts follow, and as you run out onto the street, more gunshots. You see a policeman walking along the riverfront and call to him. When he turns to answer, you see it's Boris, the policeman you met when you first woke up in Petrograd!

"Boris, come quick," you cry. "They've shot Rasputin!"

Boris looks at you at first as if you're crazy. When he recognizes you, he says, "Stay calm and tell me what the devil you're talking about."

Just then a car bursts out of the Moika Palace driveway and goes careening down the street.

Turn to page 94.

"Okay, let's call Madame Kolodnia," you say to Ilya. "I guess I don't mind going over there in the daylight, just at night."

Ilya calls Madame Kolodnia and arranges for an emergency consultation. An hour later you and Ilya are back at her doorstep, ringing the bell.

Madame Kolodnia is an exotic, red-haired woman, dressed in bright colors and jangling with jewelry. She leads you upstairs to a drawing room filled with dark icon paintings, symbols, and weird objects you can't quite figure out. After you're seated, she says, "Tea, anyone?"

"Yes, please," Ilya says. You nod mutely.

A few minutes later Madame Kolodnia brings in a tray with tea and sweet cakes. Then she sits back and waits for you to speak.

You start telling her about the events of last night, the words tumbling out of your mouth. She holds up her hand and says, "Wait, wait. Go back to the beginning, and tell me every single detail from last night. Speak slowly, and don't leave out a thing."

You take a deep breath and start over, giving Madame Kolodnia a full account of the whole night.

Turn to page 54.

"How much do you want for the boot?" you ask the man.

He quotes you a price. "That's way too much," you say.

You bargain back and forth until finally he says, "That's my final offer. I can't go any lower."

"I don't have that much money," you tell him. "I'll have to try to raise it from other Americans."

"Do so," he says. "It will be worth your while. Meet me back here with the money at three o'clock tomorrow."

You return to Ilya's apartment to find the police there waiting for you. They know you've gone to meet someone, but you manage to convince them that he never showed up. "I'll call if I hear from him again," you promise.

Turn to page 81.

You stealthily make your way through the snow-covered imperial park, moving through wooded areas whenever you can and hiding behind the many obelisks, monuments, and triumphal arches dotting the grounds whenever you see a sentry or policeman.

Soon you have found a wood near Anna Vyrubova's house, where you stop to consider your final plans. With a sigh of relief you heave the rucksack off your shoulders and sit down against a tree. A tranquil silence pervades.

Then you hear something ticking. You look at your wrist, but you're not wearing a watch. You look around, wondering where it could be coming from. Then you realize it's coming from your rucksack!

You rip open the rucksack. Your shoe box is ticking. It has been sealed with wax. Fyodor must have planted a bomb inside!

You control your feeling of panic and try to decide what to do. If you just leave the shoe box there and go on to look for Rasputin in Anna Vyrubova's house, the bomb may go off and implicate you in an attempt to assassinate the czarina. But if you try to get it off the grounds as quickly as possible, it may go off in your hands.

If you leave the shoe box and go to find Rasputin, turn to page 99.

If you try to get the bomb out of there as quickly as possible, turn to page 88.

You soon find yourself at the door of the Moika Palace, a very grand stone structure near the river. Iliodor explains that this is one of the three palaces in Petrograd owned by his patron, Prince Yussupov. When the doorman sees Iliodor, he smiles and says, "Come in, please, you have arrived just in time to take dinner with the prince."

As you walk down the marble hallways, you gasp at the luxury of the palace. You see rooms decorated with rich oriental rugs and famous paintings, tables topped with gold snuffboxes and crystal bowls full of uncut sapphires, emeralds, and opals. Iliodor whispers to you that you're in for a gourmet meal. You can't complain about that—you're starving.

Turn to page 59.

"Okay, stop," you plead. "I'll give you back the boot." At this point you'll promise anything to stop the advance of this apparition, even if you don't know what he's talking about.

As quickly as you can, you back into Ilya's room, slam the door, lock it, and head for the fire escape outside her window. But as soon as you open the window, two men in trench coats grab you.

"You're under arrest," one of them says. "Where is the boot!" he snarls, taking you back into Ilya's apartment. There you find the apparition laughing and taking off his makeup.

"We're KGB," the man in the trench coat informs you. "That boot is an historical artifact. It was once Rasputin's boot, but now it belongs to the Soviet people. You'd better turn it over."

"I don't know anything about any boot," you insist. But you suddenly remember the man outside Madame Kolodnia's and the shoe box he was clutching!

"Ah, but you just admitted you do."

"I was lying," you say weakly.

You're taken down to headquarters for interrogation. You finally convince the authorities that the man at Madame Kolodnia's never gave you the shoe box. They cross-check your story, and with the information you give them, they are able to locate and arrest the man with the shoe box.

However, they still don't let you off the hook completely—they merely deport you. Your trip to Russia has not exactly turned out as you expected it would.

The End

You quickly switch the wineglasses, give Rasputin a wink, and go back upstairs.

A few minutes later, Yussupov comes up the stairs. A full wineglass is in his hand. He walks right over to you and says, "I was very rude downstairs. I didn't offer you any wine. Please, drink up."

You have a feeling you know which glass he is waving in front of you, so you say, "No, thank you."

"I've had my eye on you the whole time. Did you really think you were any match for me?" he says, a slight sneer crossing his face. "Your plan almost worked, but you forgot one thing. The painting I was looking at had a glass cover. And glass reflects."

He sets the wineglass down on the table and gestures to his cohorts. They grab you, wrap you up in chains, and take you outside. This time when you're thrown into the Neva, you won't come out.

The End

ABOUT THE AUTHOR

JAY LEIBOLD was born in Denver, Colorado. He is the author of many books in the Choose Your Own Adventure series, including *Beyond the Great Wall*, *Secret of the Ninja*, the sequel *Return of the Ninja*, and *You Are A Millionaire*. He lives in San Francisco.

ABOUT THE ILLUSTRATOR

STEPHEN MARCHESI graduated from Pratt Institute. He has illustrated many books for both children and adults, including *You Are A Superstar*, and *Blood on the Handle* in the Choose Your Own Adventure series. His drawings have also appeared in magazines, textbooks, and children's educational publications. Stephen Marchesi currently lives and works in Bayside, New York.

Coming in March from
R.A. Montgomery—

TRIO: REBELS IN THE NEW WORLD

It is the year 2015. After decades of international war and destruction, the United States has splintered into two battling territories. It's up to three daring teenagers, code-named Trio, to help protect the free and democratic Turtalia from conquest by the Doradans—and their evil dictator Arthur Gladstone!

Book One: *Traitors From Within*

There are traitors in Turtalia, and Trio is the prime suspect! It's up to Trio to find the real mole in Command—but will they have enough time?

For the last two days Trio had followed the Doradans into a box canyon. The only way out was back the way they had come, or up. Mimla had smelled a trap from the first step into the canyon, but Matt and David had been anxious to keep on the Doradans' trail. They had seen the Doradans establish a radio-navigation site on the south wall of the canyon and had been moving closer to inspect it when they were discovered. That was only hours ago. Now they were climbing for their lives up and out of the canyon on its steepest face.

Three bullets snapped through the dry Colorado air, chipping the rock below and to the left of Mimla. Shards scattered about her, one cutting her slightly on the forehead. The superficial wound bled heavily, and she had to wipe her eyes to see. She lost her hold on the rock and slipped, but Matt held her from above and David from behind.

"Come on, hurry!"

Book Two: *Crossing Enemy Lines*

Arthur Gladstone and ruthless war contractor Lasswell Hawkins are joining forces in a diabolical attempt to take over the Northeast territory. It's Trio's mission to infiltrate Hawkins's deadly, drug-crazed army and foil the plan. But are they too late?

"Well, we know Gladstone's been in contact with some of these outlaws in the East," Matt replied to Mimla. "And we're here to find out what he's up to, if we can, besides helping the people at Prickly Mountain with their problem—whatever it is."

"I wonder if it could have anything to do with the death enzyme virus that showed up in California," Dave ventured. "That must have Gladstone scared, since he's trying to make that region part of Dorado."

"We'll find out soon enough," Matt said. "Right now we have that Cessna to worry about."

The small, hornetlike Cessna had been flying under the cloud cover, waiting for them to emerge. The pilot turned in their direction and fired off several shots.

"Something's wrong with the ailerons," Matt said. "I'm losing control!"

Reacting quickly, Mimla turned off the engine.

"Good work," Matt said. "We may as well not power into this crash. Dave?"

"Yes, Matt."

"Buckle your seat belt."

They heard a series of coughing sounds, then the tip of the right wing suddenly dangled from a fiberglass thread.

"Someone is taking this plane apart," Matt said grimly. "I can't hold it much longer."

"Down there," Mimla said. "Near the river. I saw a flash of metal."

"I thought they were friendly," Dave muttered.

"We'll soon find out."

"Hang on," Mimla said.

Then the plane hit the earth.

TRIO: REBELS IN THE NEW WORLD
Look for all six books in this new action-packed adventure series!